NIGHT AT THE MUSEUM

NICK'S TALES

NIGHT OF THE DRAGONS

NIGHT AT THE MUSEUM

NICK'S TALES

NIGHT OF THE DRAGONS

Written by
Michael Anthony Steele

Based on the book by Milan Trenc
and the motion picture written by
Robert Ben Garant & Thomas Lennon

BARRON'S

Dedication

Thanks to Kevin Ryan for the idea and for first asking the question,
"Hey... didn't the night guard have a kid?"

Night at the Museum ™ & © 2010 Twentieth Century Fox Film Corporation.
All Rights Reserved.

© 2011 by Barron's Educational Series, Inc.

Written by Michael Anthony Steele
Based on the book by Milan Trenc and the motion picture written
by Robert Ben Garant & Thomas Lennon

Cover art by Michael Okuda

All inquiries should be addressed to:
Barron's Educational Series, Inc.
250 Wireless Boulevard
Hauppauge, New York 11788
www.barronseduc.com

Library of Congress Catalog Card No.: 2010037888

ISBN: 978-0-7641-4672-5

Library of Congress Cataloging-in-Publication Data

Steele, Michael Anthony.
  Night at the museum nick's tales : night of the dragons / written by Michael
Anthony Steele.
      p. cm.
  "Based on characters created by Milan Trenc, Robert Ben Garant & Thomas
Lennon."
  ISBN: 978-0-7641-4672-5
  I. Night at the museum Nick's Tales. Title.   III. Title: Night of the dragons.

PZ7.S8147Nj 2011
[Fic]—dc22   2010037888

Date of Manufacture: December 2010
Manufactured by: Command Web Offset, Jefferson City, MO

PRINTED IN THE UNITED STATES OF AMERICA
9 8 7 6 5 4 3 2 1

**When Nick turned the corner, he spotted
his father right away...**

Larry was at Czar Nicholas's display area.
The czar was gone but Nick's dad was still
there.

As Nick approached, he realized something
was wrong. His father was standing inside
the alcove and he wasn't moving. He was
standing there as if *he* were one of the museum
displays.

"Dad?" Nick asked.

When Nick got to him, he saw that his father
was *exactly* like the other displays. His eyes
were glassy and his skin had the bright sheen
of hard wax.

"Dad!" Nick said, grabbing his father's arm.
It was cold and hard as a rock...

CHAPTER 1

Nick Daley's sneakers slapped the granite floor as he sprinted down the wide corridor. His echoing footsteps were swallowed by the sounds of his pursuers— stomping boots, creaking leather armor, and rattling scabbards. Panting, the young boy chanced a look over his shoulder; the warriors were gaining. He turned back and poured on the speed.

The enemy wasn't only behind him. Nick barely dodged an attack from the right. He ducked under flailing arms and grabbing hands. Clutching his cargo to his side, Nick slowed as another attacker launched from the left. Nick pushed off the ground and leaped over the now-horizontal adversary.

Nick allowed himself a smile. The end of the hallway was only a few yards away. He was almost there! He was going to make it!

That was when the twelve-foot-tall woolly mammoth stepped into his path.

The enormous beast lumbered in from an adjacent hall. She trumpeted loudly and wrenched her head around. Nick skidded to a halt as long ivory tusks whizzed by his face. Turning back, Nick saw that his pursuers were almost upon him. The boy ducked under the beast and scrambled between the mammoth's tree-trunk legs. As his pursuers crouched to follow, the woolly mammoth swatted them away with her long trunk. The warriors tumbled across the floor.

Once on the other side of the beast, Nick sprang from his crouch and dashed to the end of the hallway. When he reached the intersection, he raised his cargo high over his head and then slammed it to the floor. The football bounced erratically as a whistle blew nearby. Nick smiled as Theodore Roosevelt, twenty-sixth president of the United States, raised his arms high into the air, signaling a touchdown. The former president blew the whistle once more.

"Bully!" roared Teddy Roosevelt as he slapped the boy on the back. "Well played, Nicholas."

"Thanks, Mr. President," Nick replied.

Just then, Nick's pursuers gathered around him.

"Hoota, milla-woota!" shouted Attila the Hun. The angry warrior pointed at Teddy, then up to the woolly mammoth. "Winga saaaaaaaaa-ma noto!"

The other four Hun warriors stood with their arms crossed and angry expressions on their faces.

Teddy shook his head. "It was a fair play. At least according to our improvised hallway rules." He patted the mammoth's large haunch. "You should've chosen Lily for your team this time."

Lily raised her trunk and trumpeted.

Attila snatched the football from the floor and loomed over Nick. The leader of the Huns glared down at the boy as he shoved the ball toward him. "Neema tanga da mitoo foota wo-halla," he growled in the long-dead language.

Nick took the ball but held his breath in anticipation. He had no idea what the angry warrior had just said.

"Attila thinks the game would be more challenging if one had to transport a real pig," Teddy translated. "Instead of a mere pigskin-covered ball."

The Hun sneered a little longer before bellowing laughter. He tousled the boy's short brown hair. Relieved, Nick let out his held breath. However, before he could catch another, Attila playfully slapped him on the back—hard. Coughing and doubling over, Nick waved a hand at the Huns as they marched away.

As Nick gasped for air, Teddy put on his hat and long riding gloves. His tan Rough Riders uniform was once again complete. "You know, when I was president, I insisted new rules and regulations be created to make football safer," said the former president. "Of course, I didn't have Hun warriors in mind back in 1905." His iconic toothy grin spread across his face. "Or woolly mammoths, for that matter."

There was only one place in the world where a former president of the United States could referee a football game played by ancient conquerors and a long-extinct land mammal. It was the same place where an active Mayan civilization sat next to a diorama of ancient Rome—each having inhabitants less than four inches tall. It was the same place where a bronze statue of Christopher Columbus could casually *stroll* past a giant replica of a stone head from Easter Island—a head that consistently pestered anyone and everyone for chewing gum. There was only one place in the whole world where these kinds of things happened every night. That place was the Museum of Natural History in New York City.

Nick and Teddy headed for the stairways leading from the second floor to the main hall. Like the rest of the museum, the giant foyer was three stories high. Tall columns surrounded and supported the cavernous room. Two sets of marble staircases at the back of the hall led to the second floor. Separate stairs in the back of the second level led to the third. Both second and third floors had railed walkways where visitors could overlook the lobby below. Various other rooms and corridors branched off these walkways. The museum was very big and full of activity.

In the main hall, various historical figures mingled and walked through a zoo of wild animals. A zebra and gazelle trotted past Sacajawea, the Shoshone Indian scout who worked with American explorers Lewis and Clark. She was holding a conversation with two Vikings. Sacajawea wore a beaded buckskin skirt; the Vikings wore heavy furs and held battle-axes. Sacajawea glanced up and waved at Teddy and Nick. Then she and the Vikings sidestepped as a tyrannosaurus rex skeleton lumbered by. Rexy was chasing one of his own fossilized rib bones across the floor. The bone was being dragged by a string connected to a toy dune buggy. Riding in the car's passenger seat was Octavius, a tiny Roman soldier figurine from the diorama room. A miniature cowboy named Jedediah drove the toy car.

As Teddy and Nick descended the stairs, the car skidded to a stop in front of them. "Look out there, partners," warned Jed. "Big bony stampede coming through!"

The car's tiny tires peeled out as it accelerated and drove away. Rexy tromped by, snapping at the bone with his tooth-filled mouth. Both Teddy and Nick ducked as his bony tail whipped overhead.

At the main information desk, the museum's night guard talked with a real Egyptian pharaoh. The pharaoh, Ahkmenrah, dressed in his shimmering tunic and robes, was the reason all of this was possible. Inside his chamber in the Egyptian wing was a magical gold tablet—the Tablet of Ahkmenrah. It was this tablet that allowed all of the museum's occupants to come to life every night.

The night guard, dressed in his gray uniform, was the reason why Nick Daley was able to experience the magic of the museum. The night guard was Larry Daley, Nick's father.

After his parents' divorce, Nick's father bounced from job to job, never taking anything too seriously. It was only after getting the night guard job at the museum that Larry finally took charge of his life. He soon left the museum to become the CEO of his own company. However, after many of the exhibits were transferred to the Smithsonian museum in Washington, D.C., Larry set off to rescue them. It was during that adventure that he realized he was happiest as a night guard in the museum. Nick was happiest there, too. He enjoyed hanging out with his dad at the museum. And he had grown quite attached to all the historical figures.

Nick and Teddy approached Nick's father and the pharaoh.

"Of course you're welcome to get on the Internet in McPhee's office," his dad told the pharaoh. "Just don't tell the Neanderthals. They've barely mastered fire so I think pop-up ads will really freak them out."

Larry noticed Nick and Teddy. He put a hand on his son's shoulder. "Hey! So, how was the big game?"

"I won," said Nick with a smile. "Again."

"And the Huns didn't chop the ball in half this time," added Teddy.

"That's my boy." Larry beamed.

"Well, dawn approaches," Teddy announced. He gave a nod to each of them. "Nicholas, Ahkmenrah, Lawrence." The former president strode over to his display stand. There, his horse—named Texas—pawed at the floor with one hoof.

"So, Nick, how have you enjoyed your first day of summer vacation?" asked Ahkmenrah.

"My first day was great," Nick replied. "But my first *night* was better."

"Yeah, Nick is going to have to adjust his sleep schedule," said Larry. "If he's going to come to work with me every night this summer."

Ahkmenrah sighed. "Ah, the young can adapt so quickly," he said. "If I were but a few thousand years younger..."

Nick laughed. Even though the pharaoh was thousands of years old, he looked several years younger than Nick's father.

Larry checked his watch. "We're getting close to sunrise," he told Ahkmenrah. "Will you help me get everyone headed back to their spots?"

"You'd better move them quickly," Teddy advised. The former president sat on his horse, high atop his display pedestal. He aimed his large binoculars toward the front doors and windows. "We're about to have company."

Larry, Nick, and Ahkmenrah dashed to the revolving door and peered through the glass. In the predawn light, they saw a taxicab pull to a stop in front of the museum. A short, heavyset man stepped out. He wore a gray overcoat over a brown suit with a matching bow tie. It was Dr. McPhee, the museum director.

Dr. McPhee knew everything about the museum. He knew all the historical facts about every statue, display, and figure. He knew absolutely everything about each exhibit . . . except for the small fact that those exhibits came to life at night. Nick swallowed hard. Now the director was going to find out just how special his museum really was.

CHAPTER 2

"Can you stall him, Nicky?" Larry asked his son.

"I'll try," Nick replied.

"Thanks," said his dad before sprinting away from the door. "Okay, everyone," Larry shouted. "We have a code red! I repeat... we have a code red!" He began ushering all of the exhibits out of the main hall. "Sorry to cut the night short but you know the drill, folks."

Ahkmenrah helped Larry guide the animals and historical figures up the stairs and into the various adjoining halls and corridors. After most of them were gone, Nick turned his attention back to McPhee. The museum director marched up the marble front steps, digging through his pants pocket. He pulled out a ring of keys and began thumbing through them.

Nick glanced back to see Rexy taking his rightful place on a wide display stand at the front of the hall. The T-Rex skeleton struck a pose that had him facing the front doors with his mouth wide, as if in midroar. The skeleton nodded his head ever so slightly in Nick's direction and then took his original pose. Nick thought that if the dinosaur still had eyes, it would have just winked at him.

Nick turned back as McPhee reached the door. "Hi, Dr. McPhee," Nick shouted through the glass. "I'll get it." He reached for the latch on the door.

McPhee sighed and dropped his key ring back into his pocket. He watched as Nick struggled with the door lock. Of course, Nick wasn't really struggling. He only pretended so he could give his dad more time to get everyone back into their places.

"I think it's stuck," Nick said, and he faked putting more pressure on the latch.

The director rolled his eyes and shoved a hand back into his pants pocket. He pulled out the keys and thumbed through them. "Here, let me," he said with a British accent.

He shoved the key into the lock and Nick felt the latch begin to turn. He added more pressure, keeping it still.

"You need to let go now," said McPhee.

"I'm trying to help," said Nick. "I think it needs oil or something."

"Well, then turn it left," McPhee instructed.

Nick applied more pressure against the turning latch. He could still hear animals moving around upstairs.

"My left or your left?" Nick asked, hoping to stall the man a little bit longer.

McPhee's brow furrowed. "Your left, of course. Why would I tell you to turn it to my left?"

"So, is that counterclockwise?" asked Nick. He still fought the turning latch with his hand.

"Right," McPhee agreed. He used both hands to turn the key.

"My counterclockwise or your counterclockwise?" asked Nick. He just needed to stall a few
more seconds.

"Son, if this is some kind of joke, it isn't very
funny," said McPhee.

Nick didn't hear any more sounds behind
him so he slowly relaxed his grip on the
latch, letting the door unlock. When McPhee
pushed through the door, Nick was a little
out of breath. He didn't have to pretend
that part.

"Where is your father?" asked the director.

"Right here," replied Larry Daley as he
moved down the stairs. "I thought I heard
a noise so I had to" he twirled a finger in
the air behind him "inspect the... uh...
perimeter."

"Well your son played a childish prank
on..." McPhee began.

Larry interrupted the director. "Nicky, did
you help Dr. McPhee with that rusty lock the
way I asked?"

"Yeah, uh... it was really bad this time,"
Nick replied.

"I was going to write a note to maintenance before I left," said Larry. "Let them know all about it."

The museum director looked from Larry to Nick and then back to Larry. "Right..." he said, eyeing them suspiciously. "Well, anyway, the noise you heard probably came from the loading dock. I'm expecting a delivery." He marched across the main hall. Larry and Nick followed.

Nick bit his lip as he saw a long sharp object poking out from behind a kiosk. It was Rexy's fossilized rib bone. The bone was mostly hidden, but McPhee was headed right for it. The way the man was moving, he would probably trip over it.

"Dr. McPhee," called Nick.

The director stopped and turned. "Yes?"

Nick thought for a moment, then fell to a crouch. "I just have to tie my shoe first." He quickly untied one of his sneakers and began retying it.

McPhee stared at him for a moment, mouth open. Then the director moved closer. "Thank you so much for making that announcement, Master Daley," McPhee said sarcastically. "I don't know about your father but *I* was anxiously awaiting the word that you would be adjusting your footwear for the long journey over to the loading dock. A journey, I should point out, that *you* don't have to make. In fact, you should remember that I'm only allowing you to be here at night out of the goodness of my heart. And that heart can change, Master Daley, if I find out that you're making fun of me or putting me on in any way. Do I make myself clear?"

"Yes, sir," Nick replied.

As Dr. McPhee lectured, Nick had made eye contact with his father and then glanced down at the large rib bone. Larry picked up the bone and untied the string around it. He hid it behind his back before the director turned around.

McPhee shook his head. "I see the apple doesn't fall far from the tree." He marched past Larry, toward the back of the museum.

Larry tossed the bone to Nick and then ran to catch up with McPhee. Once they were out of sight, Nick ran up to Rexy. The skeleton wagged its long bony tail.

"Forget something?" Nick asked the bony T-Rex.

Rexy lowered his head and wagged his tail faster. Nick held out the bone and Rexy snatched it up with his mouth. He bobbed up and down happily before bending around and connecting the bone back to his spinal column.

"Well done, Nick," Teddy whispered, trying to remain still. "McPhee is right. The apple *doesn't* fall far from the tree. But *I* mean that as a compliment."

"Thank you, Mr. President," said Nick, smiling.

Teddy gave him a wink, then raised his saber high. When the first beams of the rising sun streamed through the large arched windows, Teddy froze in place. During the day, he was merely a wax figure—an ordinary museum exhibit like all the others.

Nick caught up to McPhee and his father at the loading dock in the back of the museum.

Four workmen in blue jumpsuits unloaded two large wooden crates from the back of a truck. One of the men handed McPhee some papers on a clipboard to sign.

"Wait a minute," said the director. "Is that it? There should be at least six crates. Not just two."

"That's all we have," said the workman. He extended a finger to the clipboard. "I think the others got delayed."

"Delayed?" asked McPhee. "How can they be delayed? And, more important, when will the rest of them get here?"

"We just move 'em," the other man said. "We don't schedule 'em."

The director sighed. "Fine." He scribbled his name across the top page on the clipboard. The men closed the back of the truck and drove off.

"New exhibits, huh?" Larry said once the truck was gone.

"Nothing gets by you," said McPhee. "You're wasting your time here as a night guard. You should be lead detective at Scotland Yard."

Nick barely paid attention to Dr. McPhee's snotty remark. He was more curious as to what was inside the two crates. Both were a good foot taller than his father and very wide.

Larry grabbed two crowbars from a nearby workbench. He handed one to McPhee and they began prying the front from one of the crates. Nick stepped back as the lid fell forward. Packing peanuts poured out, but there was nothing inside.

"Wait a minute," said McPhee. He reached to the top of the crate and swept away more foam peanuts.

It only seemed like the crate was empty because the figure was shorter than the wooden box itself. As the director pulled out more packing, a young girl's face appeared. The two men carefully pulled her the rest of the way out of the crate.

Nick had always done well in history class. And since his father started working at the museum, he had done *really* well. However, he didn't recognize the new mannequin at all. She was a young girl, about twelve years old, the same age as he was. She wore a plain brown skirt with a simple white apron. She had on a dark green blouse, and her long brown hair was pulled back into a simple braid.

"Oh, this is all wrong," said McPhee.

"What is it?" asked Larry.

"She wasn't supposed to be ready until next month," said the director.

"I don't get it," said Nick. "Who is she?"

The director swept a hand toward the mannequin. "*This* is Joan of Arc."

"Really?" asked Larry. "I knew she was young, but not this young." He moved in for a closer look. "And I thought she cut her hair and wore shiny armor and all that."

"Yes, yes, and yes," agreed McPhee. "But this is part of a special display I commissioned called…*Destined for Greatness*." He waited for Larry and Nick to say something. When they remained silent, he continued. "You see, I wanted to inspire today's youth with these new characters, showing that they, too, can be great." He smiled at Nick. "Now…don't you feel inspired?"

"Uh...I guess so," Nick replied.

The director rolled his eyes. "Well, it doesn't matter for the moment," McPhee continued. "She's early anyway." He began to pry the other crate open with the crowbar. Larry rushed in to help him. "Hopefully, *this* will be part of the temporary exhibit I've been waiting for."

When the front was removed, packing peanuts spilled out like before. This time, they revealed a man's face. Piercing blue eyes stared out of a gap in the foam nuggets. The director and Nick's father excavated the large mannequin from the hundreds of foam bits.

The man wore an elaborate military dress uniform. A dark blue coat matched pressed slacks. Several medals adorned the left side of his chest, and each shoulder bore a decoration made of tassels of gold rope. In his hand was a wooden cane. The bone handle bore two intricately carved dragons entwined around a large clear crystal.

However, the mannequin's decorative uniform contrasted against his facial features. The man, obviously very important, wore a black beard that seemed a bit too long and unkempt. The man's hair was slicked neatly to one side but seemed greasy and somewhat dirty. Nick thought the man looked familiar. But even with his newfound interest in history, he didn't recognize the new figure.

"May I present, on loan from the Royal Belgium Institute, Czar Nicholas II of Russia," said McPhee. He paused for a moment before thumbing through the shipment's order form. "I was supposed to have the entire royal family," he explained. "There should be eight of them total, including his most well-known daughter, Anastasia."

"Oh yeah," said Nick. "We just read about them last year in world history. The royal Romanov family from Russia."

McPhee raised an eyebrow. "I'm *almost* impressed, Master Daley." He brushed away a few more packing peanuts from the mannequin's dress uniform. "Of course, having just one member of the royal family doesn't make for such an impressive display, I'm afraid."

Nick gazed at the czar's pale blue eyes, which for a split second seemed to move. Of course, that was impossible. Nick knew that the mannequin wouldn't come to life until sunset. However, Nick felt uneasy as he stared at the new exhibit. He couldn't decide what it was, but there was something that didn't seem quite right.

CHAPTER 3

After a good *day's* sleep, Nick and his father returned to the museum. The sun hung low in the sky, and traffic on the streets and sidewalks began to thin. As they entered the museum, they found the cleaning crews finishing up their duties. They also found Dr. McPhee waiting for them.

"Mr. Daley, great to see you!" The museum director was uncharacteristically friendly as he put an arm around Larry's shoulders.

"Uh... hi," said Larry.

"Listen, Mr. Daley, the czar Nicholas display isn't drawing the kind of crowd I'd hoped for," McPhee explained. "He's front and center of the Hall of Eastern Europe, but no one seems to notice him. And those who do, keep asking, where's Anastasia? Where's Anastasia?" He glanced around, then drew Larry closer. "Listen, do you think you can work your... magic?"

"Magic?" asked Larry. He glanced nervously to Nick and then back to the director. "What do you mean?"

"Oh, you know," McPhee said as he adjusted Larry's tie. "Like you did when you first arrived. Really draw in the crowds."

Nick knew what McPhee meant. Back when his father first had the night guard job, the old night guards tried to rob the museum. They let most of the exhibits escape in the process. Luckily for the museum, Nick's dad really came through. He thwarted the robbery and managed to get all the exhibits back before sunrise. During the process, however, several things happened that the public perceived as publicity stunts. There were giant T-Rex tracks in the fresh snow—thanks to Rexy. There were cave paintings in a subway terminal—thanks to the Neanderthals. And someone even got video footage of some of the Neanderthals waving a burning torch on the museum roof.

"And I'm not talking about that after-hours business we tried," McPhee explained. "The added utilities alone cost us an arm and a leg. And, to be quite honest, some of your animatronics didn't seem quite lifelike. And many of the actors weren't very believable. No offense."

Nick stifled a laugh. He knew exactly what the director was talking about. After his dad and the exhibits returned from their trip to the Smithsonian, they tried extending the museum hours past sunset. That way the public would be there when the displays came to life. Of course, no one knew the *actual* exhibits came to life. Everyone believed the museum was full of clever robotic creatures and actors playing historical figures.

"I'll… uh… see what I can do," Larry replied.

McPhee beamed. "Brilliant!" He waved a hand. "No pressure. And nothing too expensive. Just, maybe, if something comes to you…" The director patted him on the back before returning to his office.

Nick smiled up at his dad. "No pressure, huh?"

After McPhee and the others left for the day, Larry and Nick split up and went through their usual routine. They had to make sure the museum was empty and clear of any lingering patrons that might have been missed.

Nick and his father also had to lock up a couple of parts of the museum. Nick's dad did a great job of getting everyone to get along with each other. However, simple reasoning didn't work on everybody. They still had to lock up the Hall of Insects and Arachnids—otherwise there would be bugs and spiders everywhere. They also had to lock up the temporary exhibits in B-Wing. Nick shuddered at the thought of those inhabitants roaming free.

Nick met back up with his dad downstairs. "So, who should we welcome first?" asked Larry.

Nick thought for a moment. "I guess it depends on who can cause the most trouble."

Larry held out both hands, palms up. "Let's see, Russian czar... French farm girl..."

Nick laughed. "Russian czar, definitely."

The two found Czar Nicholas II on the second floor. He stood frozen in a large display alcove in front of the Hall of Eastern Europe. The alcove was obviously large enough to accommodate several people, so the lone figure seemed somewhat out of place.

Nick glanced at his watch. Any second now.

Somewhere, in another part of the museum, a lion roared and birds squawked. Nick felt the floor vibrate as Lily, the mammoth, began to roam. He looked up at the czar. The man blinked and looked around.

Nick's dad extended a hand. "Hi, Czar Nicholas," he greeted. "I'm Larry Daley and this is my son, Nick." The czar didn't acknowledge them.

"Actually it's short for Nicholas," said Nick. "Just like you."

The czar didn't reply or shake Larry's hand. He gripped the handle of his carved cane and glanced around in confusion.

"Czar Nicholas?" asked Larry. He snapped his fingers a couple of times. "Hello? Your majesty?"

"Why do you keep calling me that?" asked the czar. He spoke with a thick Russian accent.

"I'm sorry, is there some other title you prefer?" asked Larry.

"I am the great"—he pounded his chest and the medals clinked; he seemed surprised and looked down to inspect his uniform—"Nicholas." He ran his fingers across his medals and silk sash.

"Just Nicholas?" asked Larry. "Seems a bit casual, but all right."

The czar's head snapped up. His eyes now clear, all hints of confusion were gone from his face. "Czar Nicholas II at your service." He clicked his boot heels together and gave a curt bow.

"Okay, hi… again," said Larry. "I'm the night guard here at the museum." Larry rubbed his face. "Gee… I've never had to explain this before."

Nick stepped up. "Sir, there's this magical tablet that brings everything in the museum to life."

The czar looked as if he were about to move away from Nick but then stopped. "Magical tablet?" the czar asked. "This... tablet is why I am... conscious?"

"Yes, sir," Nick replied.

"Very interesting," said the czar. His Russian accent made the V sound like a W. It sounded as if he said "*wary* interesting."

The czar reached down and tousled the boy's hair. "You must tell me all about this tablet," he said, before wiping his hand on his uniform.

"We can do better than that," said Larry. "We'll introduce you to Ahkmenrah. It's his tablet and he can tell you all about..."

Suddenly a scream sounded from the floor above. It was the piercing scream of a young girl.

Nick and his father exchanged a look. "Joan of Arc," they said in unison.

Nick led the way as they sprinted down the hallway toward the stairs. The screams grew louder as they dashed up the steps. When they rounded the corner toward Joan's display, Nick spotted the young girl cowering just inside her alcove. Her display was designed to look like a field of wheat. Joan held a wooden-handled hoe in front of her.

Just outside her diorama was Ming, the Chinese jade lion. Ming was quite safe but he was also quite big—the size of a large stocky pony. Nick could tell from the lion's body posture that Ming just wanted to play. He bounced around like a giant bulldog puppy. Unfortunately, Joan didn't know he was harmless.

Nick and his Dad split up. Larry moved in on Ming while Nick moved toward the girl. He raised his hands, trying to calm her. She dropped the hoe and charged him. She grabbed his shoulders and spun him around to face the lion. Using Nick as a shield, she cowered behind him and pointed at Ming.

"What is that horrible thing?" she asked. Her French accent made the question sound like "what ees zat orreeble zing?"

"He's just a statue," Nick replied. "His name is Ming. He just wants to play."

"Statues don't move," said Joan. "Or play!"

"If it's in this museum, it does," Nick replied.

"Tell you what," said Larry. "I'll find something for Ming to do. Why don't you show Joan around, okay?"

Nick sighed. "Okay, Dad."

Nick wasn't very good at talking to girls his own age—let alone frightened historical figures. He had thought that since she wasn't a real girl, at least like the girls at his school, it would be easier. Boy, was he wrong.

After Larry led Ming away, Nick unclasped the girl's hands from his shoulders and turned around. "Hi. My name is Nick."

"I am Joan," the girl replied. She didn't meet his eyes. Instead, her eyes kept darting around the museum hallway.

"I guess this is all kind of weird, huh?" he asked. He then went on to explain where they were and how the Tablet of Ahkmenrah brought everyone to life each night.

"This is some kind of sorcery," accused Joan.

"Sorcery?" asked Nick. He shook his head. "No! No, not at all. Well... uh... yes. I guess it is. But... the good kind." He beckoned for her to follow. "Let me show you."

Nick took Joan on a tour of the museum. He explained how it was full of historical figures from around the world. He first introduced her to Teddy Roosevelt and Sacajawea. As Teddy extended an open hand, the young girl immediately shrank behind Nick again.

"Come now, dear," said Teddy. "Just because I have a larger-than-average smile, doesn't mean that I bite."

Sacajawea playfully slapped Teddy on the arm and shook her head. She leaned toward Joan. "It's a pleasure to meet you, Joan."

Joan timidly took her hand. "What part of the world are you from?"

Sacajawea seemed taken aback by the question. "Um … here. In North America."

Joan nodded to Teddy. "And him?"

"The same. The good old U. S. of A." Teddy replied. He pointed toward the main door. "This actual city, in fact. Well… that's not entirely true. I was actually manufactured in a factory in…"

Nick waved a hand. "Uh, Mr. President… can we not get into all of that just yet?"

Teddy smiled and nodded. "Quite right. Good idea, Nicholas."

Nick cringed when he glanced up and saw Attila and the other Huns marching toward them.

Teddy caught his gaze and spotted the approaching warriors. He quickly intercepted the Huns and spoke quietly as they huddled around him. Nick could feel Joan's grip tighten on his shoulders as they broke from the huddle and walked toward them.

Attila reached down and gingerly took Joan's hand. "Ka-nowato wootoo," he said. He gave a small bow before leaving with his warriors in tow. Nick couldn't believe it. That was the most calm he had ever seen the Hun. Way to go, Teddy! he thought.

"I think he said he's happy to meet you," Nick translated. Or at least that's what he hoped the ancient warrior said. Teddy gave a small nod.

"I suppose *they* are not from here," said Joan.

Nick laughed. He pictured Attila and his warriors commuting on the subway. "No," he said. "No, they're not."

Joan peered out the front windows. "How big is this city?" She stepped out from behind him and moved toward the front door.

"Uh... it's really big," he said. "I'd show you but you can't go outside."

"Why not?" she asked.

Nick tried to think of a nice way to explain how she would turn to dust if she were caught outside the museum after sunrise. Not surprisingly, the words didn't come to him.

Luckily, he didn't have to explain. Rexy tromped by and Joan dived, screaming, behind the information desk. Once the giant skeleton was gone, Nick took her arm and helped her to her feet. "That's Rexy. He's harmless," Nick explained. "Although he does play a bit rough sometimes."

Joan was too frightened to respond. She had crept back into her shell.

Nick led Joan back to the second floor and showed her the Hall of African Mammals. She seemed a bit more at ease meeting Dexter and the other capuchin monkeys. However, she was careful to keep Nick between her and the lions on the other side of the large room.

As Nick showed her around the museum (most everything but B-wing), Joan hardly said a word. Nick tried his best to strike up a conversation.

"So, you led the French army, huh?" he asked. "I bet that was really cool."

"I did no such thing," she said. "I live on a farm in the village of Domrémy."

"Oh, that's right," said Nick. He remembered that she was part of McPhee's new *Destined for Greatness* display. "You haven't done that yet." However, he didn't know how this girl could possibly lead anyone into any battle. She was scared of everything. He knew the museum and its live inhabitants were a lot to take in, but the others seemed to adapt very quickly to their surroundings. Why didn't she?

He took her around to meet Jedediah and Octavius and showed her the other miniature civilizations in the diorama room.

"Howdy, miss," greeted Jed.

"Good evening," Octavius added. They both stood atop the seat back of a long wooden bench.

Joan's eyes widened as she leaned closer. "Look! They are so small."

Jed took off his hat and slapped it to his leg. "Well, heck. That's not very nice at all."

Octavius nodded. "Agreed."

"What do you mean?" asked Joan.

"What do I mean?" repeated the tiny cowboy. "I mean that I just met you, so I didn't come right out and say something about your enormous size. That would have been rude."

Octavius nodded again. "True. Not nice at all."

"Wait a minute," said Nick. "You call my dad Gigantor all the time. You call me Mini-Gigantor."

"Ah! That's different, my liege," Octavius pointed out. "We've been through battle together."

Joan leaned closer. "My size is just fine, you know," she snapped. "I am normal size. It is *you* who are tiny."

"Tiny?!!" shouted Jed. He shook his head at Octavius. "Aw, she went and done it! She called me tiny!" The little Roman held Jed back as he tried to push forward.

Nick ushered Joan away from the bench. She pushed against his arms as if she were ready to scuffle, too. "Uh, guys, cut her some slack," he told the miniatures. "It's her first night, okay?"

"I don't care what night it is," said Jed. "You don't just up and call a fella the T-word!"

Jedediah was still shouting as Nick led Joan out of the diorama room. He couldn't believe he actually had to avert a fight between Joan of Arc and a tiny cowboy figurine. Just another night at the museum, he supposed.

Nick continued the tour through the planetarium, the reptile wing, and even the insect wing. Joan wasn't a big fan of all the slithering, crawling, and scurrying exhibits. Nick felt as if his shoulders would be bruised by the way she clutched them so much from behind him.

Nick and Joan ended up at the entrance of the Ocean Life wing on the third floor. A large plastic wall of water was lit with moving lights to give the effect of a rolling wave. A door led through the center of the structure.

"This is one of my favorite parts of the museum," Nick told her. "But it may be a little overwhelming at first."

"I always wanted to visit the ocean," she said. It was the first positive thing she said all night.

"Are you sure?" Nick asked.

Joan took a deep breath. "Yes," she replied. "I want to see."

"Okay," said Nick. She was finally beginning to show some bravery.

Nick opened the door and they stepped through. They stood on the balcony of another large hall. During the day, dolphins, manta rays, and all kinds of whales were suspended on wires over the hall. At night, however, all of these sea creatures swam through the air above as if they were in the center of a giant fish tank.

Nick glanced over and saw Joan's eyes wide with a smile stretched across her face.

"I told you it was cool, right?" he asked.

"Cool?" Joan looked at him, puzzled. "It feels just as warm in here as everywhere else."

Nick was about to explain what he meant when the great blue whale rose into view. Its eye was the size of a dinner plate and stared right at them. Joan's smile disappeared as the whale boomed a loud whale song. A jet of water burst from its blowhole and salt water sprinkled down on them like rain.

That seemed to be Joan's breaking point. She didn't grab Nick's shoulders and shield herself like she had before. This time, she simply ran back through the exhibit door, screaming at the top of her lungs.

Nick gazed into the whale's giant eye—its expression now seemed slightly offended. "Sorry," he apologized. "She's new."

Nick hurried to catch up with Joan. He finally found her downstairs, crouched inside her alcove. No matter what he said, he couldn't get her to budge.

Nick went looking for his father. He checked out Ahkmenrah's chamber and found Czar Nicholas talking with the pharaoh. They were in the back of the chamber, pointing to the golden tablet. The tablet, not much bigger than a laptop, was mounted on the wall. Two corners were broken away and six spinning squares lined its face. Each square was etched with a hieroglyphic symbol.

"Hi, guys," he said to the twenty-foot jackals standing guard just inside the chamber. The dog-faced warriors nodded as he passed.

"That is all quite intriguing," said the czar.

"Yes, it is," Ahkmenrah agreed. "I've never met someone so interested in how the magic actually works, though."

"Excuse me," said Nick. "Have you seen…"

The czar rounded on him. "Children should not speak until spoken to," he barked. His pale eyes were wide with anger.

"Uh… I'm sorry," said Nick.

The czar's eyes darted to the pharaoh and then back to Nick. His face lightened. "Forgive me," he said. "You startled me, young man."

"That's… okay," said Nick, a little confused by Nicholas's attitude. He turned to Ahkmenrah. "I was just wondering if you've seen my dad."

"I have not, Nick" said the pharaoh. "He introduced the czar and me and then went on his way."

"Okay, thanks," said Nick.

As Nick made his way to the exit, he glanced back to see one final glare from the czar. The man caught his eye and quickly turned back to Ahkmenrah.

"So, would you say the magic is metaphysical or astronomical in some way?" Nicholas asked.

Nick found his father in the main hall at the museum entrance. He was chatting with Teddy Roosevelt. The former president had his jacket off and was brushing Texas the horse.

"So, what do you think of our new guests?" asked Larry.

"Czar Nicholas is ... strange," Nick replied. "But the big problem is Joan. She didn't make a very good first impression with Jedediah.

"Well, that's hard for anyone to do," said his dad.

"Yeah, but other than that, she's scared of *everything*, Dad."

The boy shook his head from side to side. "I don't see how she could go on to lead an entire army."

"Nick, my boy, I once gave your father some very important advice," said Teddy. He stopped brushing Texas and picked a few hairs from the brush. "Some people are destined for greatness…"

"And others have greatness thrust upon them," Larry finished. "Yes, I remember very well."

"So Joan fits into the *destined for greatness* category," said Nick. "But I think she has a long way to go."

"Maybe she needs someone to show her the way," Teddy suggested.

Larry's eyes widened. "Hey! And that person is you, Nicky!"

Nick winced as his dad clutched his shoulders. Yep, they were sore already. "I don't know, Dad…"

"Come on, you're perfect for the job," said Larry. "You're both the same age…"

"Give or take a few hundred years," Nick pointed out.

Larry waved the thought away. "Close enough. Look, I can't help Joan and take care of the museum. You would really be doing me a favor."

"Your chance for greatness, Nick," Teddy added.

"Great," said Nick, with a sigh.

CHAPTER 4

The next afternoon, before he and his father went to the museum, Nick surfed the Internet. He scanned several pages about the life of Joan of Arc. Unfortunately, most of what he found was about her life *after* she had fulfilled her destiny. He read about how she heard inspirational voices while working in the field. And when she was seventeen, she put on a suit of armor and led much of the French army to many victories against the English during the Hundred Years' War. Of course, he also read about what most everyone knew about Joan of Arc—the fact that she was burned at the stake several years later. Nick didn't plan to tell *their* Joan that part.

Unfortunately, Nick couldn't find any information that could help him inspire more confidence in the girl. He knew she wasn't the real Joan of Arc and wouldn't really go on to lead French soldiers in battle. But Nick didn't like the fact that she was terrified of everything. That was no way to spend every night of magical life in the really cool museum.

"You ready, Nicky?" his father called from outside his room.

"Just about," Nick replied. He almost forgot the other task he had assigned himself.

Nick did a quick search on Czar Nicholas II. He clicked on a promising-looking web link and the man's photo appeared. The uniform was dead-on but the face didn't look the same. The mannequin makers didn't get the face right on their czar Nicholas—at least according to the portrait on that particular web page. He scanned the text. His coronation was in 1896... his wife ... family, including his daughter, Anastasia... an adviser named Rasputin... He knew most of that stuff already.

There was a knock on his bedroom door. "Let's get moving," said his dad. "We don't want to miss sunset."

"All right," Nick replied. He shut down his computer and followed his dad out. He'd have to finish his research later.

When they reached the museum, Dr. McPhee was already gone. The last of the cleaning crew was packing up as Nick followed his dad downstairs to the security office and locker room. Larry grabbed his key ring and flashlight from his locker. "You want insects or B-wing?" his dad asked him.

"B-wing, I guess," replied Nick. "It's closer to Joan."

Larry patted him on the back. "You'll be great," he said as he walked out. "And you better hurry." He tapped his watch. "Almost time."

Nick trotted up the stairs, heading for B-wing. It was on the third floor, around the corner from Joan of Arc's display. As he darted up the last flight, amber light faded from the nearby window.

Keeping a brisk pace, he jogged past Joan of Arc's alcove when a shriek nearly ruptured his eardrums. Clasping his hands to his ears, he turned to see Joan screaming. She looked around and seemed to remember where she was. Her scream faded and her mouth slowly closed.

"Sorry," she murmured. "It would seem that I'm not yet used to this... coming to life." She backed against the wall and clasped the wooden handle of her hoe. She eyed the other exhibits as they walked by.

Nick bit his lip and took a deep breath, waiting for his heart rate to slow. "That's it," he said, marching toward the nearby supply closet. He rummaged around until he found a dingy mop and bucket. He pulled the mop out and set it on the ground. Placing his foot on the mop head, he unscrewed the handle. Once it was free, he strode back to Joan.

"Here." He held the mop handle out like a sword. "What's the French phrase... *en garde*!"

Joan raised an eyebrow and climbed out of her alcove. "That is not a sword," she said. "And your French is not so good."

Nick reached out with his handle and lightly tapped her hoe handle. "Yeah, well, you get the idea." He struck her handle again, this time a little harder. "Listen, you're supposed to lead the French army in battle. You should know how to sword fight."

"I told you all of this before," she said. "I don't plan to lead anyone anywhere."

Nick waved her away and turned toward the sound of clanking footsteps. Two medieval suits of armor marched by. "Hey, fellas. A little help?" The knights halted and looked his way but remained silent. "Do you think you can show us some cool sword-fighting moves?"

The knights turned to each other and drew their swords. Nick and Joan jumped back as the knights began to fight. The blades clanged loudly as they swung their weapons and then blocked each other's attacks.

Nick waved his hands. "A little slower, guys," he instructed. "We just want to learn the basics."

The knights looked at each other, then to Nick, then back to each other. One knight raised his sword as if striking a downward blow. The other raised his in a defensive posture. They both froze in place.

"Okay, this is good," Nick said as he grabbed Joan's arm. He ushered her toward the two suits of armor. Nick positioned the hoe in her hand to where the tip of the handle was like the tip of the sword blade. He raised her arm until she was mirroring the posture of the defensive knight.

"I really don't think..." Joan began.

"Trust me," Nick reassured. "This'll be a confidence builder."

Nick then moved around and raised his mop handle until he took the same position of the attacking knight. "Okay, what's next?" he asked him.

The attacking knight slowly brought down his sword while the defending knight raised his. In slow motion, the defending knight blocked the attacker's blade.

"Okay, just do what they did," Nick instructed. He slowly brought down his mop handle while Joan raised hers. The handles clicked quietly as they hit.

"Great," said Nick. He looked over at the knights. "What's next?"

Suddenly, the defending knight crouched and spun. Taking the attacker off guard, the defender swung his blade around, knocking the attacker off his feet. He crashed to the ground.

"Okay, I think that one's a little complicated for this..." Before he could finish, he glanced up to see Joan making the same move. Her wooden handle knocked his feet out from under him. Nick landed right next to the sprawled knight.

Joan laughed. "You were right. I do feel better." She turned to the knight standing beside her. "Thank you very much, monsieur."

The knight nodded but made no reply.

"Do you not speak?" she asked.

"Uh, Joan..." Nick began as he got to his feet. "They're suits of armor." The knight raised his visor, revealing no one inside.

Joan's hoe fell to the ground with a loud rattle. Then Joan's eyes rolled back and *she* fell to the ground.

"Oh, boy," said Nick. He had his work cut out for him.

He was about to help her up when he heard a commotion nearby. A loud growl and the sounds of clanking metal echoed down the hallway.

"B-wing!" he said. He forgot to lock up B-wing!

Nick sprinted down the hallway. When he turned the corner, he saw the six Civil War soldiers in the heat of battle. The soldiers were really faceless, cloth mannequins used to show off their Union and Confederate uniforms and gear. When Nick's father first got the security job, the soldiers constantly fought one another. Now they were fighting together. With bayonets affixed to the ends of their rifles, they battled an unseen foe through the doorway leading into B-wing. Nick knew what they were battling and he hoped he wasn't too late. Another loud growl rumbled from inside.

Nick sprinted harder, then slid to a stop. Unfortunately, the freshly waxed floors kept him sliding further than expected. He slid right into the fray. Nick spun his body as a sharp bayonet jutted in from one direction. Then he ducked as a razor-sharp talon slashed from the other.

Once past the doorway, he grabbed for the thick wooden door. The soldiers kept prodding the rifles through the doorway as the door swung around. They kept the creature on the other side as Nick slammed the door shut. Two of the soldiers put their backs against the door as Nick went for a large key jutting out of the door. He spun the key, locking the door in place.

"Thanks, guys," Nick told the soldiers as they stepped away. They saluted in reply as he leaned against the pounding door, catching his breath. "That was close."

Nick returned to find Joan sitting in her alcove. He knelt beside her. "Are you all right?"

"I feel so stupid," she said. "I just don't know how I'll get used to this place."

"That's easy," Nick replied. "Just be ready for anything."

Joan frowned. "Now, how can I do that?"

Nick shrugged. "I don't know. But it's a lot of fun trying."

As Joan got to her feet, Dexter scampered down the hallway. The capuchin spotted the boy, then darted to intercept. It wasn't until the monkey got closer that Nick saw two tiny figures riding on his back. It was Octavius and Jedediah.

Nick knelt down. "What's up, guys?"

Jed tipped his hat to Joan. "This is kind of an emergency, but, first of all, I'd like to apologize for getting all riled up last night."

"My apologies, as well," said Joan. "I didn't mean to call you names."

"Thank you kindly, miss," the little cowboy replied. "Name-calling has never done anybody any lick of good." Jed turned to Nick. "We have big trouble, Mini-Gigantor!"

Nick rolled his eyes and sighed. "What kind of trouble?"

"It's the new guy," said Octavius. "Czar Nicholas. We saw him walking about... during the *daytime*!"

Dexter chirped and nodded his head in agreement.

"Wait a minute." Nick shook his head. "Two things... number one... it's impossible for him to move in the daytime. And, two... you guys can see what's going on while you're frozen?"

"Oh, sure," said the tiny cowboy. "We've been watching you giants for years."

"It's true," Octavius agreed. "I'm sure it's all part of the magic of Ahkmenrah's tablet." Again, Dexter nodded in agreement.

"How can the czar move during the day?" asked Joan.

"Aw, come on, guys," said Nick. "It must've been someone else."

"I assure you, we are not mistaken, my liege," said Octavius.

Nick stood. "Well, I know one way to find out. Let's go to the basement."

Dexter climbed onto Nick's shoulder as he and Joan walked to the elevator. After the doors opened and they stepped inside, Nick turned to Joan. "Now, don't freak out. This is called an el-e-va-tor..."

Joan socked his arm. "I rode in one yesterday," she said. "Mechanical boxes I can handle. Faceless knights and moving statues are going to take some getting used to."

Nick rubbed his bicep. "Okay... just checking."

They rode down to the basement where Nick led them to the security office. There were two video monitors showing black-and-white, grainy footage from two security cameras. On both screens, Nick saw all the exhibits moving around, playing games, socializing—pretty much the opposite of what you would expect from museum exhibits. Luckily, Nick's dad was the museum's only security guard and the only one who would have any interest in reviewing recordings.

Nick found the correct machine and rewound the video feed. He watched all the figures move backward to their own spots in the museum. Then they froze in place. After a bit of time where only the cleaning crew was present, Nick saw a few museum patrons walking backward. The crowd grew as he rewound the video to show the events happening earlier that day.

"There he is!" shouted Jedediah. He pointed to the video screen.

Nick stopped rewinding and let the video play forward at normal speed. Sure enough, he saw the czar moving through the crowd. He could only see him from behind, but his uniform was unmistakable. Plus, he carried the same wooden cane.

"I don't believe it," Nick muttered.

Joan smirked. "What did you say about being ready for anything?"

CHAPTER 5

"I don't believe it," Larry said as he leaned closer to the video monitor. Nick had fetched his father as soon as he saw the czar on the video playback. He rewound the video and played him the same scene.

"Well, believe it, Gigantor," said Jed. "How does this guy get away with that, anyhow?"

Nick's dad stopped the playback and stood. "I don't know," he said. "But I'm going to find out."

With Dexter riding on his shoulder, and with Jedediah and Octavius riding on Dexter's back, Nick and Joan followed his father upstairs. Luckily, they didn't have to go far. They found the czar on the mezzanine, overlooking the main entrance hall.

"Uh... excuse me, your czarness," said Larry. "All of us have this burning question to ask you."

Nicholas raised an eyebrow. "Yes?"

Larry scratched the back of his neck. "You see, all the other exhibits here are frozen during the day and only come to life at night," he said. "So how is it that you, alone, get to walk around during the daytime?"

Czar Nicholas squeezed the head of his dragon cane with both hands. "I don't know what you mean."

"We saw you!" yelled Jedediah.

"Yes," Octavius agreed. "What would you say here, Nick? Oh, yes... you, sir, are so busted."

The czar's eye twitched as he held the cane tighter. "I, too, am frozen during the day hours," he said. "The same as you." He gestured to Joan, Dexter, and his passengers.

"That's not what they saw," said Larry.

"Well, they are mistaken," said the czar.

"Are you calling them liars?" asked Nick.

Fury flashed in Czar Nicholas's eyes. He opened his mouth to speak, then slammed it shut. After he seemed to compose himself he said, "I wouldn't dream of calling them liars. I'm merely guessing that they saw someone else."

"We saw, too," said Joan. "On that video screen... thing."

"That fancy get-up of yours tends to stand out," Jed added.

"What shall I tell you?" the czar asked. "It was not me." A grin spread across his face. "I can no more walk the daylight hours than you, my honorable companions."

There was a tense moment where nobody said a word. Finally, Nick sighed. "All right," he said. "If you say it wasn't you, then it wasn't you."

"What?" asked Joan.

"Ah, come on, Mini-Gigantor," Jed whined. "My eyes don't lie!"

"Nor mine, my liege," Octavius agreed. Dexter chirped in agreement.

Nick's father looked at Nick and nodded his head. "You know, guys, I think we should believe the czar. He's new here and there's no reason for him to lie to us."

"Thank you," said the czar. He clicked his boot heels and gave a quick nod.

"Come on," said Larry. He led Nick and the others away. "Sorry to bother you, your majesty."

"Not at all," said the czar. He shot a quick glare to Nick and Joan before turning and walking away.

When they were out of earshot, Nick asked "Are you thinking what I'm thinking, Dad?"

"You mean, thinking of being a couple of turncoat, snakes in the grass!" said Jed. "How can you take his word over ours?"

"Yes, I don't understand," said Joan.

Larry knelt in front of the group. "Come on, guys, you know me better than that," he whispered. "Look, Nick and I will take care of him tomorrow morning. Don't worry."

Octavius beat his chest with his fist—a centurion's salute. "Never doubted you for a second, my liege."

Jed rolled his eyes. "Suck-up."

The next morning, after all the exhibits returned to their displays, Nick and Larry unlocked everything as usual. What they didn't do as usual was go home. Instead, they grabbed a pair of walkie-talkies from the security station. They knew better than to stake out the czar's display directly. If the Russian knew they were onto him, he would simply stay still until they left. They also had to avoid Dr. McPhee. He'd want to know why they had stuck around during business hours.

Nick and his dad agreed to split up and stay at opposite ends of the museum for a while. Once enough people came through, they would blend into the crowds to see if they could catch the czar walking around.

Nick hung out in the Ocean Life wing under pods of suspended dolphins and whales. His dad camped out in the planetarium. Both places were darker than the rest of the museum and made it easier to blend into the background.

Thirty minutes after the museum opened, the hall began to fill with patrons.

"Now, Dad?" Nick asked into the radio.

"I have a thin crowd over here, but it should be enough to cover us," Larry replied. "Let's do it."

Nick began to blend with the crowd. He followed a group out of the Ocean Life wing and into B-wing. He didn't bother scanning the two exhibits that were giving them so much trouble. They would be frozen in place like the others. Instead, he scanned the crowd, looking for the one exhibit that somehow *was* able to move after sunrise.

Once back in the main corridor, a dark shape caught his eye. Nick bobbed between two tall patrons to see a man at the end of the hallway. Even though Nick only saw him from behind, it was clear who it was. The man wore the unmistakable dark blue coat with a white silk sash. Golden-roped decorations rode on each of his shoulders.

Nick smiled. "Gotcha!" He held up the radio and keyed the transmitter. "I found him."

"Where?" his dad's voice asked.

"Third floor, heading toward petrified wood," Nick replied.

"I'm coming," said Larry.

Nick pushed through the museum patrons, trying to close the distance between him and the czar. Unfortunately, he had to detour around a group of rowdy kids. When he finally rounded the corner, he spotted the czar descending one of the back staircases.

"He just went down the south stairs," Nick reported. He hurried to catch up.

"Copy that," said Larry.

When Nick made it to the second floor, he spotted Czar Nicholas gliding through the crowd at the end of the corridor. Then he disappeared into the Egyptian wing.

Nick keyed the radio. "Dad, he's going for the tablet!"

He didn't wait for his father to reply before he broke into a run. He darted around more kids and tourists. He turned the corner leading into the Egyptian wing. As he ran toward Ahkmenrah's chamber, his dad emerged from a nearby stairwell. They both burst into the pharaoh's chamber at the same time.

The chamber was empty of patrons except for an elderly man and woman making their way toward the exit. However, at the end of the chamber, next to Ahkmenrah's sarcophagus, was Czar Nicholas. The man stood with his back to them as he gazed up at the tablet.

Nick and Larry let the couple exit before moving in on the czar. Larry got there first and grabbed one of the man's arms. He spun the czar around.

"I thought you said..." his voice faded off.

It was Dr. McPhee. The museum director wore a simpler version of the czar's dress uniform. A fake bushy beard and mustache adorned his face—an *obviously* fake beard and mustache.

"Dr. McPhee," said Nick. "Why are you dressed like Czar Nicholas?"

"I think the answer is pretty obvious, don't you?" the director asked.

Larry cocked his head. "You like wearing... or dressing as..." He shook his head. "I got nothin'."

"I'm trying to drum up some excitement for the new exhibit," McPhee explained. "I asked you to come up with something but you didn't, did you?" He smoothed out his uniform jacket. "So I took a cue from the Larry Daley guerrilla advertising playbook, as it were." He looked up and smiled. "Pretty good, eh?"

Nick and his father nodded vigorously. "Oh yeah. Sure. Absolutely," they said.

Larry backed away. "We just thought some kids were messing around. But we see you have it well in hand. We're just going to go home now."

Nick followed his dad. "Yeah ... kids," he told the director.

When Nick and his dad were outside the Egyptian wing, they burst into laughter.

"I can't believe Jed and the guys were fooled by that," said Nick. "I can't wait to tell them tonight."

Larry wiped a tear from his eye. "Yeah, we better get home. This little mission cut into our sleep time."

Nick and his dad made their way toward the main entrance. They kept snickering and cracking each other up along the way. Nick was still giggling when they passed the real Czar Nicholas display. Sure enough, the mannequin was still there, frozen in place.

Yet, as Nick turned away, he thought he caught a movement from the corner of his eye. It was minuscule, as if the czar blinked or something. He stopped and stared at the man. He saw only the stiff figure staring back.

"What is it, Nicky?" his dad called back to him.

Nick hurried to catch up. "Nothing," he said. "I'm just sleepy, I guess."

CHAPTER 6

The next day, Nick and his dad got to the museum early enough to run into Dr. McPhee as he was leaving.

"I just got off the phone with the Belgians," he reported. "I spoke with a lackey, but I believe we can expect the rest of the czar's family tomorrow."

"I'm sure he'll be very..." Larry began before quickly correcting himself. "I mean *I'm*... I'm very happy about that."

"All right," the director said as he gave Larry a puzzled look. "That was strange... but... but I'm glad *you're* happy. After all, that's what we all strive for around here." Dr. McPhee shook his head and dashed out the door.

"Nicky, can you lock up B-wing and all that?" Larry asked. "I want to apologize to the czar as soon as the sun sets."

"Sure, Dad," Nick replied. He was glad that *he* didn't have to explain things to Czar Nicholas.

Nick had plenty of time to lock up the insects, reptiles, and B-wing. Then, just after sunset, Nick headed toward the mammal wing to tell Dexter about what they discovered. As he passed Czar Nicholas, his father was still there.

"So, the good news is that your family should be here tomorrow," Larry told him.

"What family?" the czar asked.

"You know… your wife… kids…" Larry replied.

The czar's eyes squinted and then widened. "Oh yes. Of course!" He tapped his cane on the floor.

Nick hurried on his way, but not before catching a glaring look and slight sneer from Czar Nicholas.

Nick didn't know what it was with that guy. It was obvious that the czar didn't like him.

Maybe the man didn't like kids in general. If that were the case, then why did he have so many of them? Of course he wasn't the real czar. But every exhibit or mannequin took on the personality of the person it represented. So why would the father of so many children hate kids?

Nick also didn't know why Czar Nicholas seemed so scatterbrained or forgetful—like the time when he first came to life. It was as if he didn't know who he was. Then again, Nick had never been there when a new exhibit came to life for the first time. Czar Nicholas and Joan of Arc were his first. Of course, Joan knew who she was right away. She might have been frightened of everything and everybody but at least she knew who she was.

Nick had spent so much time working with Joan that he totally forgot the research he had planned to do on the Romanov family. There was something bugging him, something he learned in school but couldn't remember. He didn't know what bothered him more—that missing piece of information or the way the czar treated him. Whichever one it was, there was something about the man Nick didn't trust.

Nick entered the African mammals wing, weaving through a herd of antelope, gazelles, and rhinos. He moved toward the fake jungle setting between the two doorways.

"Dexter," he called. "Hey, Dex!"

A quiet chirp led his eye toward two capuchin monkeys huddled in the back of the display. They seemed frightened of something.

"What's wrong, you guys?" he asked.

With sorrowful eyes, one of the monkeys pointed to a nearby tree. Nicky followed his little monkey finger to see Dexter hanging from a branch.

"Dexter?" he asked, moving closer.

It was clear Dexter wasn't going to answer. The mischievous monkey was frozen in place. He was in his usual daytime pose. The only thing wrong was that it wasn't daytime at all. It was night and the tablet's power should have brought Dexter to life.

"Dex?" Nick snapped his fingers in front of the monkey's face. Nothing.

Nick looked around. The rest of the animals were moving about like they did every night. He stepped outside and glanced down the corridor. Other mannequins were walking around like normal—well, normal for their special museum.

Nick was confused. How could only one of the exhibits still be frozen? Looking for a friendly face, he ducked into the diorama room. Maybe Jed and Octavius could help. But the minute he stepped into the room he knew something was wrong. The diorama room, the hall of miniatures, was usually alive with activity. Instead, all was silent. Nick moved by each scene—the Mayans, the Wild West, the Romans—they were all frozen. It was as if the sun had never set. Something was very, *very* wrong.

Nick had to tell his dad. He dashed out of the room and slammed right into Joan of Arc. The two kids went sprawling.

"What is wrong with you?" she asked. "Don't you watch where you are going?"

Nick stumbled to his feet and then helped Joan up. "I'm sorry," he said. "But I have a little emergency here."

"I have something very important to tell you," she said.

Nick jogged down the corridor. "Not right now."

Joan chased after him. "But I think you will want to know this thing."

The last place Nick saw his dad was beside Czar Nicholas. Maybe he was still there. He turned down a hallway, heading for the Russian's display area.

"Hello?" Joan said, running alongside him. "Do you hear me?"

Nick kept running. "Yeah, can we talk about this another time?" he asked. "I kind of have a problem here."

"I think this might be a bigger problem," she said.

Nick wasn't really paying attention. Was something wrong with Ahkmenrah's tablet? On Nick's first night at the museum, when the old night guards tried to steal it, one of its tiles was partially rotated. Just that one thing being out of place had kept the magic from working. It prevented everyone from coming to life. Nick could understand if that had happened again. But why would it just affect some of the exhibits?

"I really think you should know this," Joan said.

Nick sped up, trying to lose her. He was glad she was running around, getting used to the place. But there were more important things to worry about than Joan's confidence right now.

Luckily, when he turned the corner, he spotted his father right away. Larry was at Czar Nicholas's display area. The czar was gone but Nick's dad was still there.

As Nick approached, he realized something was wrong. His father was standing inside the alcove and he wasn't moving. He was standing there as if *he* were one of the museum displays.

"Dad?" Nick asked.

When Nick got to him, he saw that his father was *exactly* like the other displays. His eyes were glassy and his skin had the bright sheen of hard wax.

"Dad!" Nick said, grabbing his father's arm. It was cold and hard as a rock.

Joan caught up to him, out of breath.

"That... is what... I was trying to tell you."

CHAPTER 7

Nick snapped his fingers in front of his father's face. Larry didn't blink, move, or anything. It was as if he were part of a new *night guard* display at the museum.

Nick glanced around. "Where's Czar Nicholas?"

"I saw him before," said Joan. "He had that gold tablet with him."

Nick spun around. "The Tablet of Ahkmenrah?"

"Yes," Joan replied. "The one you said makes us come to life at night."

Nick didn't understand what was happening. Sure, the czar seemed very interested in the tablet. Nick spotted him talking to Ahkmenrah on several occasions. But how could the czar himself control the tablet? And even if he could, how could he adjust it so that just a few exhibits remained frozen? And even if Czar Nicholas could do all that, how could he make his dad, a real-life person, become frozen like a museum exhibit? Nick had to find Ahkmenrah. The pharaoh would know what to do.

Nick was about to take off when he heard a long beep.

"I think there is a bird trapped in your father's pocket," said Joan.

Nick recognized the noise. He reached into his father's jacket and pulled out a mobile phone. "It's a telephone," he told Joan. She merely stared back at him. "I'll explain later."

Nick answered the phone and Dr. McPhee spoke. "Mr. Daley?" asked the director.

"Um…he's…busy right now," Nick said as he stared into his dad's unblinking eyes. "Can I take a message?"

Suddenly, a blue beam of light shot between Nick and Joan. The light was so bright it took a second for Nick's eyes to readjust. When they did, Nick spotted Czar Nicholas at the end of the hall. He held the tablet in one hand and his cane in the other. He sneered at the kids as he raised his cane. The cane's crystal glowed blue and the tablet glowed gold. Nick got a sinking feeling. He flipped the phone shut and shoved Joan out of the way. Another beam of blue light appeared. It shot from the cane's crystal to just over their heads.

"Come on," Nick said as he grabbed Joan's arm.

He dragged her down the corridor as another beam shot past them. This one hit the bronze statue of Christopher Columbus just as he turned to see what the commotion was about. The bronze explorer remained frozen after the beam hit him. He stayed in that curious pose, no longer moving.

"What is he doing?" asked Joan as they ran.

"I don't know," Nick replied. "But we have to find Ahkmenrah."

Another blue beam whizzed past them. Nick glanced back long enough to see the czar running after them.

"Come back, you impudent boy!" growled the czar. He brought up the handle of his cane for another shot.

Nick pulled Joan around a corner as another beam shot by. This one hit a pilgrim woman as she tried to flee. The woman froze in midrun.

"This way," said Nick. "I know how to lose him."

Nick ushered her through the Mayflower room, toward a plain metal door in the back. A security keypad was mounted beside the door. Nick entered the code as Czar Nicholas bolted into the room's entrance.

"I have you now," he said, raising the cane. The crystal and tablet glowed.

Nick opened the service door and pushed Joan through. He ducked inside and pulled the door closed. Something hit the door hard and it began to crackle. His hands felt cold where he was pushing the door shut. He pulled them back just as a layer of frost crept over the surface. No doubt, if he hadn't removed his hands, they would have stuck to the metal door the same way a person's tongue would stick to a metal lamppost in winter.

Nick's mind raced, full of unanswered questions. How could this be happening? How could a Russian czar use the magic of the tablet that way? And what was with the cane? Now *it* was magical, too? Nicholas wielded that cane the way a wizard would use a magic wand. A wizard? The czar's piercing eyes came to mind. Something about that crazed expression made him think of what he studied about the Romanov family.

Nick jumped as the phone rang in his hand. He flipped it open. "I'm sorry, Dr. McPhee, we were cut off." Something slammed against the locked door. Nick motioned for Joan to follow him as he moved down the stairwell.

"Tell your father I need him to do me a big favor," McPhee said.

"Sure," Nick replied. He tried very hard not to sound as if he was running from a Russian czar with the ability to freeze anyone and anything he wanted.

"Good," McPhee continued. "Now, I know this isn't in your father's job description, but I need him to… undress Czar Nicholas."

Nick halted on the landing. "What?"

"You see, there's been a big mistake," McPhee explained. "I just heard back from Belgium and there was an accident with the costumes. They had to get them cleaned, and… well… long story short, they sent us the right costume on the *wrong* mannequin."

"Rasputin," said Nick. "That's who they sent, isn't it?"

There was a pause before McPhee answered. "That's right, Grigory Rasputin," he replied. "But how did you… oh, that's right. You studied it in school, didn't you?" The director sighed. "You know, you could have told me this before."

Nick and Joan continued down the next set of stairs. Their echoing footsteps made it difficult to hear but they had to get to Ahkmenrah. "Sorry, it just came to me, sir."

"Very well," McPhee replied. "The dragon cane is Rasputin's but the costume belongs to Czar Nicholas."

Suddenly, it all made sense. Rasputin had been the czar's adviser. And, according to what Nick had learned, there had always been a lot of controversy surrounding him. Many thought he was an evil mystic. Nick supposed it wasn't much of a stretch from mystic to sorcerer.

"Just have your father remove his uniform before morning," the director instructed. "The Romanov family, including the real Czar Nicholas, are being delivered first thing. I want to get them set up properly as soon as possible."

"Uh... okay," said Nick. "I'll tell him." Nick closed the phone and slipped it into his pocket. "*That's* why he was so curious about the magic of the tablet," he told Joan.

"Who?" she asked.

Nick explained about the mix-up and who Rasputin was. "The magic of the tablet must give him *real* magic. That's why he can use his cane to freeze everyone." Nick shook his head. "I should have been reading up more on Czar Nicholas, instead of you."

"You were reading about me?" asked Joan.

"Yeah." Nick gave her a half smile. "I was trying to figure out how to get you to be more brave. You know, live up to your reputation."

"I... I don't know what to say," said Joan. "I..."

Nick continued down the stairs. "Let's talk about it later," he said. "We have to get to Ahkmenrah. He'll know how to stop Rasputin!"

Once they were in the basement, they cut over to the elevator and returned to the second floor. The doors opened and Rasputin wasn't around. No one was around. The coast was completely clear. He and Joan slipped out and then padded down the corridor. They turned into the Egyptian wing and ducked into Ahkmenrah's chamber. Immediately, Joan grabbed Nick's arm. She put her other hand over her mouth as her wide eyes stared up. Nick followed her gaze to the two Jackal warriors standing guard.

"Oh, the Jackals," he said. "Don't worry, they're..."

Something was wrong. Both warriors aimed their long spears at Nick and Joan. It looked as if the kids were about to be skewered. Then Nick realized that the giant guards weren't moving. He and Joan backed away from the scene, and the Jackals continued to aim their spears at the same spot on the floor. The statues were frozen, too.

Joan lowered her hand and let out a breath. "He's already been here," she said.

It was then that Nick heard the rattle. They ran to the pharaoh's sarcophagus. The lid clattered and Ahkmenrah's muffled yells could be heard from inside. Nick tried to unlatch the clasps, but they were frozen solid and cold to the touch.

Joan tried the other clasp but it wouldn't budge. "Sir?" she called. "How can we get you out?"

The pharaoh yelled back but they couldn't understand what he said through the thick sarcophagus lid.

"Let's go," said Nick, tugging on Joan's sleeve. They ran out of the pharaoh's chamber. "Maybe Teddy can help us."

Nick and Joan darted out of the Egypt wing and into the main corridor. They rounded the corner, heading for the main staircases. Just before they made it, Rasputin appeared at the opposite end of the hallway.

"There you are!" he shouted. He ran toward them, raising his cane. The crystal began to glow.

Nick and Joan turned down the stairs but then were stunned at what they saw. Amassed on the main floor were the rest of the museum exhibits. African tribes' people, Eskimos, Pilgrims, and Native Americans all glared up at the phony czar. Huns, Vikings, suits of armor, Civil War soldiers, and Neanderthals all had weapons at the ready.

Teddy Roosevelt sat atop his horse in the center of the small army. He drew his saber and gave Nick a quick wink. "The cavalry has arrived, son."

CHAPTER 8

Nick felt pride at seeing his friends gathered for battle. Even Joan wasn't completely cowering behind him anymore. He stepped away from her, taking a step up the stairs.

"Give back the tablet," he ordered. "Rasputin!"

The mystic started at the sound of his name. "So, you discovered my identity." Rasputin sneered. "What a clever child. What a clever, yet impertinent, child." He took a step forward. "Did you know I had to constantly cater to the czar's little brats? It was the only way to stay in his good graces." Rasputin made an exaggerated sad face. "Oh, Rassy," he whined in a falsetto voice. "I don't feel well, make me better. Oh, Rassy, play a game with me. Oh, Rassy, I want a glass of water." His head trembled with anger. "So now I *can't stand* children!"

"You're not even the real Rasputin," Nick shouted. "You're just a mannequin that looks like him."

Nick heard Joan gasp behind him. He knew he had hit Rasputin below the belt. But maybe he could get the evil mystic to give up the tablet without a fight. He didn't want to see any of his friends get hurt.

Rasputin stared at Nick for a moment then burst into laughter. "Don't you think I know that?" he asked. "Of course I'm not the real Rasputin! The real Rasputin didn't have any magical powers. He only *thought* he did." Rasputin raised his cane and took a step forward. The crystal glowed bright red. His frizzy beard lowered, revealing a sinister grin. "But because he *thought* he had powers, this tablet gives me *real* powers."

A fireball exploded from the crystal. Nick ducked and pulled Joan down just as it whooshed overhead.

Joan screamed. "I really don't like fire," she said.

"I'll bet," Nick agreed.

"Long-range assault!" Teddy shouted.

Nick and Joan peered through the stone banister to see Sacajawea notching an arrow. She drew back her bow and let the arrow fly. Rasputin growled as he spun toward the approaching arrow. Another fireball burst from his cane and the arrow disintegrated in a cloud of ash. Sacajawea drew and shot three more arrows faster than Nick had ever seen. Unfortunately, each arrow met the same fiery fate.

Below, the four Neanderthals hooted at the sight of the flames.

"Don't like fire?" Rasputin asked. "Then how about this?" He raised his cane and a blue beam of light blasted the cavemen. When the beam was gone, the Neanderthals were frozen in place. Rasputin shrugged. "I can do this all night."

Teddy cupped his mouth with one hand. "Left and right flanks! Attack!"

The ground trembled as elephants, rhinos, zebras, and lions charged from both sides of the second-floor corridor. Rasputin turned to blast the charging animals but they were too fast. He only had time to swing his legs over the railing and jump clear. As he landed on the first floor, swords, spears, and bayonets were leveled at him.

"Shall I take your surrender, sir?" asked Teddy.

The Russian snarled. "Never!" He raised his cane and blasted the nearest Union soldier. The faceless mannequin froze in place. The rest of the exhibits charged as Rasputin backed away, blasting his attackers as he did so.

Nick pulled Joan's sleeve. "Come on; let's see if we can help."

"I don't know," said Joan, but she followed him anyway.

They made their way down to the first floor as the battle continued. The kids dodged two Vikings as they ran around to outflank Rasputin.

Even though Rasputin was heavily outnumbered, he was winning the battle. He dodged attacks, then quickly retaliated with a freezing blast. As he backed away, the mystic left a wake of frozen figures.

Nick and Joan took cover as a wayward blast shot their way. It hit an African shaman, freezing him in midstep.

"Okay, so maybe coming down here wasn't such a good idea," said Nick.

"I could have told you this," said Joan.

They crouched behind a pillar as the sounds of battle quickly died down. Nick chanced a peek where he saw all of his friends frozen in place. When the elephant and rhino began galloping down both staircases, the mystic easily froze them in place. With the beasts blocking the stairs, no other animals could descend.

Now, Rasputin was the only moving figure on the lower level of the museum. He cautiously glanced about as he glided across the floor.

"Hello? Children?" he shouted. "I think you are hiding somewhere and are afraid to come out." The Russian looked behind the information desk and then behind a group of frozen Hun warriors. "As you can see, I am all powerful. I'll soon take over the outside world the way I have taken over this museum."

Without thinking, Nick ran to the front doors. "I can't let you leave," he said. "It's my dad's job to not let anyone enter *or* exit this museum at night."

Rasputin laughed. He extended a hand atop his eyes and pretended to search. "I don't see him anywhere." He raised the cane and the crystal glowed *red*. "Tsk, tsk... it's always the children."

Something struck Nick hard. It was Joan. She dove out from cover and tackled him. They flew to the side, away from the approaching fireball.

Rasputin ran up to them before they could rise. "Ah, now I have both of you."

Before he could level the cane at them, a deafening roar filled the hall. Loud footsteps vibrated the ground. Rexy ran out of the Ice Age wing and swung his head at the Russian. The bony skull connected and Rasputin flew across the room. He tumbled to the ground, knocking down Neanderthals like bowling pins. He quickly became buried in a pile of cavemen.

Nick and Joan got to their feet. "Way to go, Rexy!" yelled Nick. The T-Rex skeleton lowered his skull so Nick could give it a scratch. Even Joan patted him on the head.

"You have your own dragon, eh?" said a voice from across the hall. Rasputin excavated himself from the pile of Neanderthals. "Let's see what I can do about that."

Rasputin raised his cane and a cloud of red smoke emerged from the crystal. It grew larger and larger yet showed no signs of dissipating. When the cloud grew over forty feet long, it began to take shape. The front of the cloud formed a horned head. It split to create a large mouth with rows of sharp teeth. Four legs and feet extended to the floor. Each foot had long, sharp talons. Two leathery wings sprouted from the beast's back. And where the smoke tapered toward the crystal, a long tail formed, whipping back and forth. The smoke solidified into the shape of a huge red dragon.

CHAPTER 9

The crimson dragon took a step forward and gave a ferocious roar. It bellowed so loudly, the front windows shattered. It made Rexy's roar sound like a growling Chihuahua. Still, the T-Rex skeleton put himself between the dragon and the kids. Nick and Joan moved back as the giant beasts sized each other up.

Rexy was quick to strike. He leaped forward and spun around, whipping his tail. The bony appendage connected, pounding against the dragon's head. The red beast stumbled and flapped its wings for balance. Wind blew over the information desk, sending brochures flying everywhere. When the dragon recovered, it whipped its own tail around, knocking Rexy across the floor. As Rexy clambered to his feet, the dragon inhaled deeply. Its crimson eyes glowed brightly.

Nick and Joan were standing behind the T-Rex skeleton. "This can't be good," Nick said. "Come on!"

The two scampered down the front hall and dove behind a stone bench. The dragon exhaled and flames engulfed Rexy. Joan whimpered as the flames lapped over the top of the bench.

When the fire died down, Nick snuck a peek. Rexy was still standing, but his bones were glowing red. The T-Rex roared loudly.

"Hmm..." said Rasputin. "Wrong sort of dragon."

He raised his cane and a column of blue smoke emerged. The smoke grew until it solidified into a large blue dragon.

Still glowing, Rexy snapped at the blue dragon. The new beast inhaled and its blue eyes flashed. Then an icy white cloud erupted from its mouth and engulfed Rexy. It was as if the skeleton was swallowed in the spray from a giant fire extinguisher. Sharp cracks sounded all over

Rexy's body. When the mist disappeared, Rexy was frozen solid. The red dragon roared and spun around, slapping the giant skeleton with its tail. Rexy shattered into a million pieces.

"No!" shouted Nick as he stood. Joan grabbed him and pulled him out of the main chamber. They ran out just as the blue dragon blasted the front of the museum with another white cloud.

Rasputin laughed as he climbed onto the back of the red dragon. The blue dragon rammed the frozen front of the museum. In an explosion of brick and glass, it tore through the front wall. Rasputin's dragon galloped out after it.

The museum lights flickered and went out. In seconds, the emergency lighting system activated. The destruction was bathed in a faint amber glow.

Nick and Joan ran back into the hall. Through the giant breach in the museum, they watched the two dragons fly out over Central Park.

Nick sat on broken stone and put his face in his hands. What was he going to do? His father and all of his friends were frozen stiff. Rexy was gone and the museum was wrecked.

"Is there no way to stop him?" asked Joan.

Nick shook his head. "I don't know how. Everyone that could help us is frozen. And even if there was someone else"—he pointed to the sky—"how can we get to him up there?"

Joan sighed and sat beside him. "This place has so many wonderful things." She picked up one of Rexy's long talons. "You even had a dragon of your own. It's too bad your dragon couldn't fly."

Nick's chest tightened. He had an idea, but that idea both excited and terrified him. "We don't have any dragons," he said as he stood. "But we might have the next best thing."

"Really?" asked Joan. "Where?"

Nick sighed. "In B-Wing."

Since the main stairs were blocked by an immobile elephant and rhino, Nick and Joan ducked into the back stairwell. They ran up to the third floor and down the main corridor toward B-wing. Nick took a deep breath before turning the key. He pulled open the thick wooden door and they stepped inside.

The large hall had very few emergency lights and seemed darker than the rest of the museum. Of course, that could have just been Nick's imagination. He was terrified of what was in the large room with them. He couldn't make out any of the exhibits. And he certainly couldn't spot the two creatures they came to see.

As if to make things worse... *BAM!* The thick door slammed shut behind them. The echo seemed to go on forever. The room seemed darker then ever and the air felt thick. Suddenly it was hard to breathe.

Something skittered behind them. Nick and Joan spun around but saw nothing. Then they heard a bump on the opposite side of the room. They turned back but all was silent. It was so quiet that Nick thought he heard his own heart beating. Joan grabbed his arm as they crept further into the room.

"Hello?" Nick called.

Two dark figures slammed to the ground in front of them. He could only make out the tall outlines of the looming creatures. He couldn't see exactly how close they were, but he could feel their hot breath on his face. And he felt their low rumbling growls more than he heard them.

"Uh, hi..." he said, trying to sound confident. "I really hate to bother you guys but we... kind of... uh... need your help."

Nick's hair blew back as one of the beasts roared in his face. Joan squeezed his arm tighter as she let out a small squeal. Nick fought every urge to get out of there as fast as he could.

"Uh... you see...," Nick continued, "there is a man, a kind of wizard, who stole this tablet that brings everyone to life each night. And we... uh... we really need to get it back." He tried to keep his voice from shaking. "I know that we lock you up here every night, but..."

The other beast interrupted Nick with an ear-splitting squawk. It clicked its sharp talons on the hard floor.

A year ago, during Nick's first night at the museum, he watched his father give a great rallying speech to all the exhibits. He got them to put aside their differences and work together to battle the old night guards. He had them fight toward a common goal. But Nick didn't have anything in common with these creatures. And he certainly didn't have practice giving rallying speeches.

"Uh… and maybe…," he continued, "so… if you help us…"

Joan let go of his arm and stepped forward. "Hello," she greeted in a shaky voice. "My name is Joan."

The first beast let out a few guttural clicks and snorted in reply.

"I'm just like you," she explained. "I'm on display in this museum. When I first awoke here, I was very frightened and confused. I didn't know what to think of all the strange things that live here." She took another step forward. "But I'm really trying to give the museum a chance. It's hard but I'm trying. And, believe it or not, the more I try, the more I think that I will really like it here." She moved closer still. "I think that if you give this place a chance, you'll like it, too.

But none of us will get that chance if we don't stop a very bad man from making it all go away. You two are the only ones that can help us."

The dark figures clicked, grunted, and snorted to each other. It was as if they were really talking it over.

Nick sidled up to Joan. "That was great," he whispered. He cut his eyes up to the looming figures. "I hope they think so, too."

CHAPTER 10

Nick held tight as they soared out of B-wing and flew down the third-floor corridors. Wings flapped as they rose over the handrail and then dipped into the main hall. They dove sharply, then shot through the large hole in the front of the museum. Nick and Joan burst into the cool night air, each riding atop their own pterodactyl!

Nick couldn't help grinning as they rose into the sky. His pterosaur extended its wings to its full twenty-foot wingspan and gave a loud squawk as it surveyed its new surroundings. Nick ducked as the back of its long pointed head passed over his. He rode upon the animal's smooth gray shoulders, with his arms wrapped around its neck. Nick leaned forward and held tight as the flying reptile flapped its leathery wings harder.

Joan's pterodactyl flew in tight formation next to his. It opened its long beak and gave an answering caw. Its rider, the girl who had been frightened of her shadow for the past few days, was actually smiling. Holding on to its long neck, her body dipped and swayed with every move of her flying steed.

Nick laughed. "You're a natural," he shouted.

"Horses," she said back. "I grew up on a farm, remember?"

Nick nodded his head. Of course.

"You ride well, too," she told him.

"Not my first ride on a prehistoric reptile," he shouted back.

Nick used to ride Rexy all the time. He'd use an Oriental rug as a saddle to cushion himself against the skeleton's hard vertebrae. Nick's smile vanished. Now Rexy was in a thousand fossilized pieces spread across the museum floor. His friend wasn't much more than a thin layer of gravel.

Anger simmered inside Nick as he scanned the skies. He spotted two faint lights high above the center of the park. One was red, the other blue. He pointed at them. "Let's get him!"

The pterosaurs beat their wings and climbed toward the enemy. As they closed in, he could see the outlines of the glowing dragons. The red and blue creatures lazily flapped their long wings, unaware that they shared the skies with other flying beasts.

Nick leaned forward. "Go for the tablet as fast as you can," he told his pterodactyl.

Not giving away their element of surprise, the animal simply grunted a reply. It beat its wings faster.

Nick gave Joan one more glance. She nodded and slipped closer to her pterosaur's neck, getting a better grip. Nick did the same just as they hit.

Ka-woosh!

Both pterodactyls buzzed between the dragons. The resulting air current sent the red and blue beasts tumbling in different directions. Rasputin yelled, trying to hold on.

"Now!" Nick yelled.

His pterosaur spread its wings wide until it halted its ascent. Then it folded its wings and they dropped like a stone. It flapped them once they were over Rasputin and the blue dragon. The pterodactyl hovered over the dragon and used its clawed feet to snatch at the tablet.

With the tablet tucked under his left arm, and his left hand holding on to the dragon, Rasputin beat at the attaching claws with the cane in his right hand. "Back, you vile demon!"

Still hovering, the pterodactyl screeched as it kept slashing and grabbing. One of its talons ripped open the mystic's sleeve. Rasputin shrieked in pain.

Then just as the tablet was in reach, Nick's pterodactyl backed off. Nick looked up just as the red dragon came flying toward him. The monster let out a roar and all he saw were rows of sharp teeth. Then Joan's pterodactyl zipped in and slammed against the red dragon. The two tumbled through the air in a tangle of sharp talons and jagged wings. For a moment, they seemed as if they would spiral all the way toward the park below. Then they split from one another, each flying in opposite directions. Nick was glad to see Joan still atop her pterosaur.

Nick's pterodactyl went back on the offensive. Below, Rasputin continued to evade the reptile's claws. He struck the talons with his cane and dodged every grab for the tablet. The pterosaur was quick and getting closer to its target with every strike. But then the blue dragon bellowed and wrenched its head around. Its eyes glowed as it inhaled deeply.

"Look out!" Nick shouted.

His pterodactyl banked just as a column of ice burst from the dragon's mouth. Goose bumps formed on Nick's arm as they dodged the freezing attack by inches. If they hadn't moved, no doubt he and his pterodactyl would be frozen stiff and tumbling toward the ground below.

"That'll teach you to respect your elders, child!" taunted Rasputin.

Nick's pterodactyl flapped its wings to gain altitude. Joan's own pulled up alongside him as the two dragons regrouped on the other side of the park. Both pairs of flying creatures slowly circled each other.

"We couldn't get the tablet," Nick told her. "And that was with a sneak attack."

"What now?" she asked.

Nick opened his mouth to reply but nothing came out. He had no idea. All he could think of was the same attack. It was two against two, except his and Joan's flying beasts couldn't breathe fire or ice. Nick racked his brain trying to come up with a plan. Unfortunately, his newfound interest in history hadn't included military strategy. But even if it did, how could you outflank someone in the sky?

"Uh... I got nothin'," he said.

Joan looked at him, then back to Rasputin. "Then I suppose, I must finally lead the charge."

"What?" asked Nick. "Wait a minute..."

She kicked the sides of her pterosaur and it moved toward the dragons. "Hold back until the time is right," she shouted at him.

"What time?" Nick asked.

"You'll know," she yelled.

Nick and his pterodactyl kept their distance as Joan charged the two dragons. He didn't like the look of this. It seemed even worse when a fireball erupted from the red dragon. Joan's pterosaur banked left and dodged the attack. Then she buzzed the dragons, flying past them and toward the city. To Nick's surprise, the red dragon turned and gave chase. It shot another blast of fire but Joan's flying reptile banked right, swerving just out of the way. The two beasts became smaller as they flew into the night.

This was the moment Joan meant. She had separated the two beasts. Now it was just Nick and Rasputin. No help from the other dragon. No distractions.

"Let's go!" Nick yelled as he kicked the sides of his pterosaur. The beast bucked forward as it accelerated toward the blue dragon.

Using the same strategy as the red dragon, the blue dragon turned to face them. Its eyes glowed and a freezing ball of ice erupted from its mouth. Nick held tight as the pterodactyl angled out of the way. They dodged two more icy attacks before they finally reached Rasputin. At the last second, Nick's pterosaur spread its wings wide, slowing it like a parachute. It whipped its feet forward, going for the tablet. Once again, the blue dragon roared and whipped its head around, trying to protect its master. This time, however, the pterodactyl pecked at it with its long beak before it could blast them.

"You horrible, horrible child!" cursed the Russian.

Suddenly, warm light flickered over them. Nick glanced up to see a fiery explosion high in the sky. Inside the blast, he could just make out the outline of leathery wings. *Booooom!* The delayed sound of the explosion punctuated the dull pain in his stomach.

"Joan," Nick murmured.

Rasputin bellowed with laughter. "You see that, boy?" he asked. "It seems that your little friend was always destined for a fiery end."

Nick trembled with rage. He had lost yet another friend tonight. His father and all the others were frozen solid and who knew if they could be returned to normal. Nick was the only one left to save the museum and he was failing miserably.

Rasputin continued to fend off the attacks from the pterosaur's claws and the dragon snapped at the reptile's long beak. Nick could no longer just sit there while everything fell to pieces around him. Without thinking, he climbed past one of the pterodactyl's flapping wings and hurled himself toward the dragon below.

Nick landed flat on the dragon's rump. The impact of the hard scales knocked the breath out of him. The dragon dipped sharply as it adjusted to the added weight. As Nick slid back toward the dragon's tail, he grasped madly at the smooth scales to keep himself from falling off. His fingers finally caught a raised scale. He held on by one hand as the rest of his body dangled off the back of the dragon.

Climbing up the dragon's beefy leg, Nick scrambled to the dragon's back. Once straddling the beast's bony spine, Nick scooted forward. He ducked as Rasputin's cane swung at his head.

"Get back, brat!" yelled the Russian.

He brought the cane up for another strike. He had to switch targets at the last minute as more of the pterodactyl's talons came at him. Rasputin opted to fend off the prehistoric beast instead of the twelve-year-old boy.

Nick moved in and jerked the tablet out from under the mystic's arm. Enraged, Rasputin growled and rounded on him with the cane. Nick ducked another blow.

"Give it back, boy!" Rasputin barked. "Now!"

Nick slid back away from the mad Russian. He had to find a way to get back onto his pterosaur. As if sensing his intent, the pterodactyl swung its head around. Holding the tablet under one arm, Nick reached for the long beak. As his fingers touched the hard surface, the blue dragon wrenched around and bit down on the pterosaur's long neck. The reptile squawked and struggled to get free. Nick and Rasputin held tight to the dragon's back as the two creatures thrashed about.

Suddenly, the world was spinning. Locked in battle, the two beasts tumbled toward the ground. City lights streaked around them as they spun out of control. Nick felt his stomach tighten and his head clouded up as he became dizzy. He held tighter to the dragon's back—the only stationary thing in his new spinning world.

Unfortunately, the only other clear object in his blurry vision was Rasputin. As Nick held tight, the man continued to inch forward. The evil mystic smiled as he brought up his cane. The tablet glowed under Nick's arm as the cane's clear crystal glowed bright blue once more. "I really *hate* children!" the man growled.

Nick glanced over his shoulder at the spinning world. Streaking city lights were interrupted by a large blur of darkness. He looked back at Rasputin and waited as long as he dared. Then, just before he thought the Russian would blast him, Nick pushed off the dragon's back. Rasputin's eyes widened in disbelief.

Still clutching the tablet, Nick tumbled through the air. He curled into a ball and hoped that what he saw earlier had been what he thought it was.

SPLASH!

Nick fell into the cool water of Central Park Lake. The heavy tablet and the height from which he fell drove him deeply into the water. When he stopped descending, he swam up to the surface. He saw a blue light above, then heard a giant *whoosh* as something very large fell into the water beside him. There was another flash of blue light.

Fighting the weight of the tablet and the weight of his wet clothes, Nick struggled to swim upward. Luckily, he was almost there. He reached a hand up to the surface and it struck something hard. Nick kicked harder and reached up again. His hand slammed against the obstacle once more. The barrier was hard and cold to the touch. The lake had been iced over.

Nick was trapped.

CHAPTER 11

Nick pounded against the thick sheet of ice. His lungs ached for air and his body was tired from swimming. Darkness began to creep into the edge of his vision. He slapped the hard ice once more. He wasn't going to make it.

KRUNCH!

Something burst through the ice above him. Nick shielded his face, then felt something very large grip his shoulders. As he was pulled from the water, he inhaled loudly, gasping for breath. He looked up to see one of the pterodactyls holding him in its claws. The winged reptile flew him to one side of the hole in the ice and then released him. Holding the tablet tight to his chest, Nick tumbled to the hard surface.

Wind blew across his face as the reptile fluttered to land beside him. Nick coughed up some lake water, then looked up and saw who was riding the pterosaur.

"Joan!" Nick cried. "You're all right!"

Some of Joan's hair was singed and curled from the fire. Her face and clothes were dotted with patches of black soot. She smiled as she stroked the neck of her equally singed pterosaur. It cooed a response.

"I saw the explosion," Nick said. "And I thought..."

"I think the beast wasn't as powerful far from its master," she explained. "If you hit it hard enough it simply... pops." She tried to smooth down some of her curled hair. "It pops into a *giant ball of flames!* I did mention that I really don't care for fire, didn't I?"

Nick looked at the ice below. That's why the lake had frozen. The red dragon went out in a fireball. When the blue dragon slammed against the water, it must have blown up and frozen everything around it.

Nick scanned the surface and saw something jutting out of it. He moved closer and saw that it was Rasputin, stuck in the ice. The man's neck, shoulder, and one arm poked out of the surface. The rest was trapped below. Unfortunately, the hand that was free held the dragon cane.

"Oh, how you brats will pay for this," he growled. Nick noticed the tablet begin to glow. "I will summon thousands upon *thousands* of dragons!" The cane's crystal glowed red. "They will fill the skies! My power will allow them to exist during the day, as well." The crystal glowed brighter. "Their spread wings will block out the sun!"

An ear-piercing squawk precipitated a strong gust of wind. Nick's pterodactyl swooped in and hovered over the Russian. It snatched the cane from Rasputin's hand and flicked it toward Nick. As the boy caught it, the crystal's glow slowly faded.

Rasputin stared at him in disbelief. "Kidding!" said the Russian. "I was just kidding you. Just a silly little game."

Nick rolled his eyes as he and Joan climbed atop their pterodactyls. The creatures' wings beat the air as they rose off the ground.

"Come back!" he cried. "I really *do* like children." He tapped his coat with his free hand. "I may have a chocolate here somewhere…"

As Nick and Joan flew back to the museum, a faint glow appeared on the horizon. It looked as if they only had a couple of hours before sunrise.

Once back inside, the pterosaurs flew up to the third floor while Nick and Joan remained in the main hall. They walked among his frozen friends, their bodies posed in attack positions. All the while, their feet crunched over what used to be Rexy.

"I was hoping…" Nick began. "I was hoping that they'd be back to normal. You know, Rasputin's spell would be broken." He plopped down on Rexy's display stand and set the tablet and cane beside him. "Now we're back to where we started. Everyone that can help us is frozen stiff."

"Why do you need help?" Joan asked. "You have in your possession two of the most magical items I have ever seen."

Nick looked at her like she was crazy. "Are you kidding? I'm not a wizard, a mystic, or even the pharaoh who owns it." He nodded to the tablet and cane. "I have no idea how to use those things."

Joan shook her head. "If you had told me yesterday that you knew how to ride a flying beast, I wouldn't have believed you." She threw up her hands. "Or that you knew how to fight an evil wizard... or battle dragons!" She aimed a finger at him. "Was it not you who told me about realizing my potential? About this big *greatness* I'm destined for?"

"Yeah, but you're ... you're Joan of Arc," he said.

Joan shook her head. "No. No, I'm not." She crossed her arms. "I'm merely a mannequin of her when she was a young farm girl." She raised an eyebrow. "Don't you think I know all about what Joan of Arc did? How she became inspired to lead great armies to victory. How she was eventually burned at the stake for what she believed."

Nick had been so stupid. Of course she knew all of that. Part of the magic of the tablet was that it gave the mannequins the knowledge and personalities of whom they represented. That was why Teddy Roosevelt could tell you everything about his presidency even though his mannequin design represented "Rough Rider" Teddy.

"And *that* is why I'm so frightened," Joan continued. "I have a lot of destiny to live up to. It's very daunting, believe me." She knelt before him. "But you... you've already seen so much and done so many incredible things." She picked up the tablet and cane. "A phony mystic who merely *believed* he was great could wield these objects." She handed them to him. "I know that someone who *is* truly great can make them work just as well."

Joan stepped back and waited. Nick looked down at the golden hieroglyphics, then to the carved dragons in the cane. The tablet felt warm and heavy. The cane seemed to vibrate under his grasp.

Nick stood and moved toward the nearest group of mannequins. Attila the Hun and his warriors had swords raised and snarls on their faces. Nick pulled the tablet tight to his chest and closed his eyes. He held the cane in front of him and concentrated. He imagined his friends as they were...moving, talking, laughing. He pictured the Huns as they were when he played football against them. A smile touched his lips and he felt the cane warm in his hand.

Nick opened his eyes to see the clear crystal begin to glow. It didn't glow red or blue, but bright gold, like the tablet. Then...it flashed!

"Woo-ta menga saaaaaaaaaaa-to watta!" Attila shouted. He and his warriors sprang to life, continuing their attack. They staggered to a halt when they realized that their enemy was gone.

"Holy cannoli," Nick muttered.

Joan laughed. "I knew you could do it!"

Attila looked around, confused. With his sword still at the ready, he marched over to Nick and Joan. "Manna setta tooku?" he asked, glancing around suspiciously.

Nick didn't speak Hun but he had a good idea what Attila had asked. "He's out there." Nick pointed toward the park. "He's stuck in the frozen lake. Can you guys go get him out?"

"Tooku fretta?" Attila asked before roaring with laughter. The other Huns joined in as they all marched out the gaping hole in the front of the museum.

Nick smiled at Joan. "Who's next?"

They moved through the main hall unfreezing the rest of his friends. Vikings, Pilgrims, Civil War soldiers, African natives, and Eskimos were all surprised and grateful to be free.

His confidence growing, Nick found he could release figures faster and faster. He unfroze the elephant and rhino simultaneously as well as the entire diorama room. Last on the first floor, he unfroze Sacajawea, Columbus, and Teddy Roosevelt. He and Joan quickly told them what had happened.

"Bully for you, Nicholas!" said the former president. "I'll expect you to regale me with the detailed account later. But first, you should see to your father. Sacajawea and I will see to cleaning up and restoring order."

"Thank you, Mr. President," Nick replied.

Teddy extended a hand to Joan. "And bully to you, too, young lady."

"Thank you, sir," she replied.

Teddy gave her a wink. "We all knew you had it in you."

Nick and Joan ran to the second floor to find his dad just as they had left him. Nick closed his eyes and concentrated on releasing his father. This one was the easiest of all. He simply thought of the love he had for his dad.

"Whoa… Nicky…" said Larry Daley. He glanced around in confusion. "What happened?"

Nick and Joan took a little longer explaining what had happened in detail. They took turns telling him about the huge battle in the main hall and then their battle over Central Park.

"Wait a minute… the pterodactyls?" his dad asked. "*The* pterodactyls? From B-wing?"

"Yeah," said Nick. "And I don't think we have to lock them up anymore." He and Joan smiled at each other. "In fact, I kind of promised that we wouldn't."

Larry beamed with pride as Nick released Dexter and the few other exhibits they missed along the way. Then they walked to the Hall of Egypt and released Ahkmenrah and his Jackal guards. Once free from his sarcophagus, Nick and Joan told the abbreviated version of their tale once more. Nick handed over the golden tablet.

"Congratulations," said Ahkmenrah. "To both of you."

The group moved to the second-floor railing to look out over the main hall. Larry whistled when he saw the devastation. "I'm not sure how I'm going to explain this."

"What is that all over the floor?" asked the pharaoh.

"Oh," said Nick with a sigh. "That's what's left of Rexy."

Nick didn't know how his father would explain the shattered skeleton to Dr. McPhee. However, that was the last thing on his mind. Nick just wanted to have his friend back. He had never owned a dog. But he knew what it was like to have a faithful and loyal friend. If he did get a dog someday, he hoped it would be a lot like Rexy. The big, goofy, skeletal lummox had sacrificed himself trying to save them. Nick was going to miss him terribly.

A commotion interrupted Nick's train of thought as the Huns brought in Rasputin. The mystic was dripping wet and strands of his greasy hair were plastered to his face. The man who seemed so menacing before shrank in stature in the custody of the Hun warriors. Joan let out a laugh and quickly covered her mouth.

Rasputin glared up at them. "How *dare* you!" he roared. "You sniveling brats!"

"What should we do with him?" Larry asked.

Ahkmenrah held up the tablet. "I can see to it that he no longer comes to life after sunset."

"You wouldn't!" Rasputin barked.

Larry nodded. "Yeah, we would. You blew your chance to play nice."

"Uh, Dad," said Nick. "You might want to take off his uniform first."

"What?" asked Larry.

"What?!!" asked Rasputin.

Nick smiled up at his dad. "Doctor's orders."

Larry shrugged and turned back to the main hall. "Attila? Huns? You heard him."

The Huns roared with laughter as they dragged Rasputin up the stairs.

"Now," said the pharaoh. He held up the tablet. "Let's see about what we can do about this destruction."

"Wait, you can fix this?" asked Nick.

Ahkmenrah smiled. "Of course. The mischief caused by the tablet can always be reversed by the tablet." He leaned over the railing. "Everyone stand clear, please."

The remaining mannequins moved away from the breach in the wall. The pharaoh raised the tablet high over his head. "Pta-Seker-Asar Ptah-Nu!" he said in a booming voice. "Pta-Disar. Ptah-Minta. Ahkmernahu!"

Suddenly chunks of brick and stone began sliding across the floor. Then they tumbled and bounced toward the opening. Piece by piece, the debris rose, re-formed, and returned to the front wall. Large shards of glass screeched as they slid across the room. Smaller pieces joined the shards as seamlessly as water flowing toward a puddle. Once the glass panes were complete, they floated up and placed themselves into the large window openings. Knots of metal strips and tubing that were once part of the revolving doors untangled and re-formed. The revolving doors rebuilt themselves inside their repaired cylinders. It wasn't long before the entire main floor looked like new. All that remained was the strewn rubble that was once Rexy.

"Too bad you couldn't restore the stone dragon," said Joan. "He fought most bravely."

Ahkmenrah smiled. "Ah... wait for it..."

As with the building debris, bits of the T-Rex skeleton began to converge. It was as if invisible hands were assembling the most complicated three-dimensional puzzle of all. What might have taken paleontologists years to do, the magic of the tablet was doing in seconds. It wasn't long before Rexy stood before them, almost complete. Then a single rib emerged from hiding and rose into the air. After it locked into place, Rexy came to life, letting out a loud roar.

Larry smiled and placed a hand on Nick's shoulder. Nick and Joan couldn't help but laugh.

"Rexy!" Nick yelled. The dinosaur turned and gazed up at them. Its mouth hung open as it wagged its long bony tail. "Good boy!" Nick shouted.

After sunset the next night, Nick, his dad, and Joan met with the newly arrived Czar Nicholas II, the *real* Czar Nicholas II, and his family. The czar looked much better in his dress uniform than Rasputin had. And the uniform had been restored perfectly thanks to Ahkmenrah.

The czar's family included his wife, Alexandra, their son, Alexei, and their four daughters, Marie, Tatiana, Olga, and Anastasia. The ladies all wore lacy white gowns. Anastasia wore a similar dress, and Alexei, the youngest, wore a blue and white sailor-styled shirt. The royal family stood outside their alcove while Rasputin remained frozen inside.

The new arrivals were welcomed by a small crowd, including Teddy Roosevelt, Sacajawea, Jedediah, and Octavius.

"It is truly a pleasure to be in such noble company," said the czar.

Anastasia particularly liked Jedediah and Octavius. "Dollies!" she shouted, and picked up little Jed.

"Hey, put me down!" he shouted. "I don't like being manhandled."

Octavius nodded. "It's true. He doesn't."

While everyone got to know each other, Alexei climbed back into the alcove. He tugged on Rasputin's long black tunic. "Rassy? Wake up, Rassy!"

"Uh... Alexei," said Larry. "Rassy was naughty so he can't come out and play."

"Oh, dear," said Alexandra.

Czar Nicholas rolled his eyes and leaned closer to Larry. "Probably for the better," he whispered. "He did tend to be somewhat of a bore."

131

"But I want to play with Rassy," Alexei whined.

Joan crouched between Alexei and Anastasia. "You can still play with him," she said. "Just think of him as a *really* big dolly."

Nick stifled a laugh. "Uh, yeah," he agreed. "Aren't there some extra costumes in the basement, Dad?"

Larry nodded. "You know, Nicky, I think there are. Why don't you two take them down and find a few things." He looked up at Rasputin. "I'm thinking a big sun hat with a nice long feather boa."

Nick chuckled. "Good one, Dad." He turned to Joan and the kids. "Let's go see what we can find."

As Nick led the way toward the stairs, Joan caught up to him. "After this, I'd like you to teach me that game you told me about."

"Football?" asked Nick. "Sure."

"Yes, that's the one," Joan replied. She gave a sly smile. "The Huns were very excited about choosing me for their team."

"Oh, boy," Nick said with a chuckle.

Where else in the entire world would he be able to play football against Attila the Hun and Joan of Arc? Nick Daley had a feeling that his summer break with his dad was going to be his best yet.

About the Author:

Michael Anthony Steele has been in the entertainment industry for almost twenty years. He has worked in many capacities of film and television production, from props and special effects all the way up to writing and directing.

For the past fifteen years, Mr. Steele has written exclusively for family entertainment. He began as a staff writer for the PBS series *WISHBONE*. There he co-wrote several episodes including the Emmy award-winning, full-length feature, *WISHBONE's Dog Days of the West*. Since then, he has written twenty-five episodes for the PBS series *Barney & Friends*, many home videos including five for the video series *Boz, The Green Bear Next Door*.

To date, Mr. Steele has authored over seventy children's books for numerous popular characters including: The Penguins of Madagascar, Batman, Shrek, Green Lantern, G.I. JOE, Speed Racer, Spider-Man, Garfield, and Sly Cooper.

Michael Anthony Steele can be contacted through his website: *MichaelAnthonySteele.com*.